World of Fairy Tales
Cinderella
and
Aladdin

Two Tales and Their Histories

an imprint of

WINDMILL BOOKS

New York

Published in 2010 by Windmill Books, LLC
303 Park Avenue South, Suite # 1280, New York, NY 10010-3657

Adaptations to North American Edition © 2010 Windmill Books

Editor (Arcturus): Carron Brown
Designer: Steve Flight

Library of Congress Cataloging-in-Publication Data

Brown, Carron.
    Cinderella and Aladdin : two tales and their histories / Carron Brown.— 1st North American ed.
        p. cm.— (World of fairy tales)
    Summary: A retelling, accompanied by a brief history, of the two well-known tales in the first of
    which a poor girl attends the palace ball with the help of a fairy godmother and, in the second, a
    poor boy discovers a magic lamp whose genie changes his life.
    ISBN 978-1-60754-643-6 (library binding)—ISBN 978-1-60754-644-3 (pbk.)
    ISBN 978-1-60754-645-0 (6-pack)
    1. Fairy tales. [1. Fairy tales. 2. Folklore—France. 3. Folklore—Arab countries.] I. Cinderella.
English. II. Aladdin. English. III. Title. IV. Title: Cinderella and Aladdin. V. Title: Aladdin.
    PZ8.B697Cin 2010
    [398.2]—dc22
                                        2009037516

Printed in China

CPSIA Compliance Information: Batch #AW0102W: For further information contact Windmill Books, New York, New York at 1-866-478-0556.

For more great fiction and nonfiction, go to windmillbooks.com.

Cinderella

ONCE UPON A TIME, IN A GREAT KINGDOM, a gentleman lived happily with his wife and his pretty little daughter. But sadly, one day, the gentleman's wife fell ill and died. A few years passed, and the gentleman married a lady who was cruel, wicked, and proud. She had two daughters who were just as cruel and wicked. This wicked lady hated her husband's daughter, because the girl's goodness and kindness showed up the stupidity, pride, and laziness of her own two. The day after her wedding, the stepmother ordered the poor child to do all the hard work in the house. She had to scour the pots, wash the dishes, and clean the floors. And she scrubbed and polished her stepmother's and her two stepsisters' rooms.

3

She slept in a dusty old attic, which was at the top of a narrow, dark staircase. When she had finished her work, the poor child sat in the chimney corner, among the cinders, where it was warm. That was why they called her Cinderella. She enraged her stepsisters even more, because even in rags with her untidy hair, she was a thousand times more beautiful than they were. Cinderella was very unhappy, but she was so brave that she never complained.

One day, it was announced that the Prince was having a grand ball. Cinderella's stepsisters spent weeks preparing their ball gowns, which gave the poor girl even more work, as she had to sew, iron, shorten, and lengthen their clothes.

"I," said the elder stepsister, "will wear my red velvet dress with the silver collar."

"I," said the other, "will wear my gold-embroidered cloak and my diamond tiara."

The two sisters forced Cinderella to be with them whenever they tried on their clothes, as they knew she had good taste.

"Would you like to go to the ball, Cinderella?" asked the younger stepsister.

"Oh! Please, don't make fun of me. Look at my hair and my ragged clothes."

"Cinderella is right," said the elder sister. "She would look ridiculous."

Almost anybody would have tried to get revenge for such an insult, but Cinderella took even more trouble to prepare their clothes. At last the evening of the ball arrived and the two sisters left for the palace, dressed in richly embroidered gowns glittering with jewels. From the window of her dusty attic, Cinderella watched them go for as long as she could and then, when the carriage was out of sight, she burst into tears.

From her far-off country, Cinderella's fairy godmother heard her goddaughter crying. With a wave of her magic wand she arrived in the attic.

"What is the matter, my gentle goddaughter?" she asked.

"Oh! Godmother, I would so love to go to the ball," Cinderella replied, in tears.

"Well, you shall go to the ball, and you will be the most beautiful woman there. Go into the garden and fetch a pumpkin."

A very surprised and curious Cinderella went out and cut a big pumpkin. With a wave of her magic wand, the fairy turned it into a magnificent golden coach.

"Now, my pretty child, I need a rat and some mice."

Cinderella brought a big rat and six little mice from the mousetrap. With another wave of her magic wand, the fairy turned the mice into six fine dapple-gray horses, and the big rat into an elegant coachman.

"Go back into the garden. Behind the watering can you will find six colorful lizards. Bring them to me," said the fairy. When Cinderella came back, her fairy godmother turned the lizards into smart footmen.

"Now you are ready to go to the ball," said the fairy, admiring the carriage proudly.

"I don't want to take advantage of your kindness, dear godmother, but dressed as I am I look like a beggar."

"Oh, dear! What am I thinking?" cried the good fairy, and she waved her wand again and again until she had turned Cinderella into the most beautiful princess. Her old shirt, full of holes, became a sparkling gold silk robe. Her hair was elegantly styled. Then the fairy gave Cinderella a pair of glass slippers that fit the shape of her pretty little feet perfectly. But her fairy godmother had a warning for her:

"Take care, Cinderella! There is one thing you must not forget. Before the twelfth stroke of midnight you must be home. Otherwise your coach will turn back into a pumpkin, your horses back into mice, your coachman back into a rat, your footmen back into lizards, and your clothes back into rags."

With a grateful heart, the lovely Cinderella promised that she would be home by the time the clock struck midnight. Then she stepped gracefully into her carriage, which took her towards the Prince's ball.

When Cinderella entered the ballroom, there was a sudden silence as, dumbstruck with admiration, everyone gazed at the dazzling beauty of this unknown lady. The Prince begged her to sit beside him, but then he found himself unable to speak because he was so enchanted by her. However, eventually he invited her to dance and Cinderella did so with such grace that everyone admired her even more. Then, very politely, she went to greet her sisters, who did not recognize her.

Time flew by until Cinderella heard the palace clock striking eleven. Immediately, she made a graceful curtsy and left the ballroom as fast as she could. As soon as she reached home, she called upon her fairy godmother.

"How can I thank you, dear Godmother? It was the happiest time of my life. But, the Prince invited me to a second ball tomorrow."

The good fairy was about to answer, when Cinderella's two stepsisters knocked at the front door. Cinderella went to open it for them, rubbing her eyes, as if she had just woken up.

"How late you are,
sisters!" she said,
stretching and yawning.
"We had a wonderful
time," said the younger
stepsister. "A new princess came,
who was very nice to us. She noticed at once
that we are just the people to be seen with."

"Nobody knows her name," continued the elder. "We heard that
the Prince would give everything he owns to know who she is."

Cinderella smiled and said:

"Please, sister, lend me your old yellow dress, so that tomorrow
I can go to the ball to see this beautiful princess."

"What? You go to the ball? Are you mad?" cried one.

"You'd look completely ridiculous! You would make us ashamed,"
said the other.

And giggling together, the nasty pair went off to bed.

The next evening, Cinderella's fairy godmother waved her magic wand again: she turned a pumpkin into a carriage, mice into horses, a rat into a coachman, and lizards into footmen. And she spent even more time making Cinderella's dress.

"Tonight you must be even more beautiful," said the fairy. "You will wear your hair loose. Your dress will be made entirely of lace. But you can wear the same pretty glass slippers as before."

And so Cinderella left for the ball dressed like a queen. On the palace steps, the Prince stood waiting. When he saw Cinderella arriving, he thought he must be dreaming: she was even more beautiful than he remembered. Gently, he took her hand in his and they began dancing, twirling and spinning, gazing into each other's eyes. Cinderella enjoyed herself so much that she did not hear the clock strike eleven or even half-past eleven. But on the last stroke of midnight, she tore herself out of the Prince's arms in panic and ran away like a startled deer.

The Prince ran after her and found one of her slippers on a stair: he picked it up, but the mysterious princess had vanished into the night. Cinderella arrived home out of breath, with no coach, coachman, horses, or footmen, and wearing her ragged clothes. All she had left was one small glass slipper.

When her stepsisters came home, Cinderella pretended to have just woken up and asked them if they had seen the beautiful princess again.

"Yes," said the elder sister, "but she ran away without even a good-bye."

"She ran off so fast," continued the younger, "that she lost one of her glass slippers. The Prince picked it up and he refused to dance or even speak for the rest of the evening. He just sat gazing at the little slipper in his hands."

"He is madly in love with her," continued the eldest, "and I think he will do everything he can to find her."

Indeed, the very next morning the King's messenger declared that the Prince would marry the girl whose foot fit the glass slipper. First they tried the shoe on princesses, then duchesses, then all the ladies in the kingdom, but none of them had a delicate enough foot. At last, the slipper was brought to the two stepsisters, who tried to squeeze their feet into it.

"Now it is your turn," said the King's messenger, turning towards Cinderella.

"You are joking," cried the two sisters, laughing unkindly. "Cinderella is just a kitchen maid!"

"I have my orders to try the shoe on all the women in the kingdom," replied the messenger.

He knelt in front of Cinderella and offered the slipper to her. The girl slipped her foot into it and, of course, the shoe fit perfectly. Then Cinderella took the other glass slipper out of her apron pocket and showed it to her stepsisters, who were astonished.

Then the fairy godmother arrived, and with a wave of her magic wand, she turned Cinderella's rags into a dress that was even more beautiful than the others. The two cruel sisters recognized the beautiful princess they had seen at the ball and they fell on their knees and begged her forgiveness. Cinderella hugged them and said she forgave them with all her heart. Then Cinderella was taken to the palace where the Prince immediately recognized his fair unknown princess. He found her more beautiful than ever, held her in his arms and swore to love her forever. They married and had many children.

Cinderella, who was as good as she was beautiful, brought her stepsisters to live at the palace too and, within a year, they were married to two of the lords at court.

THE END

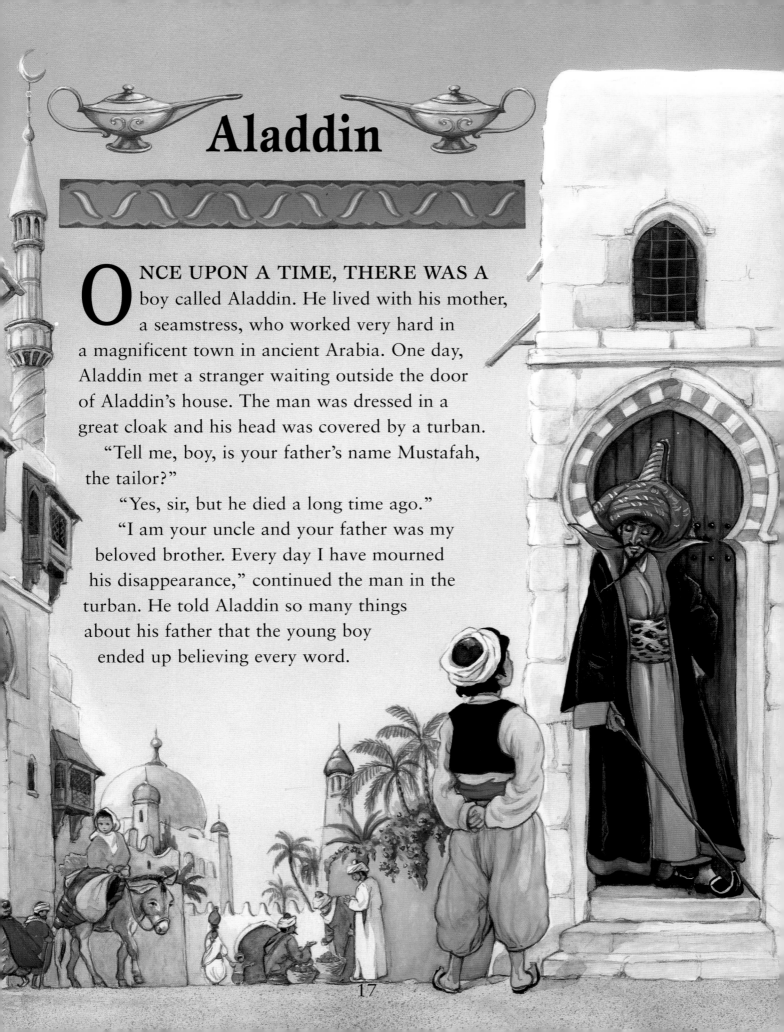

Aladdin

ONCE UPON A TIME, THERE WAS A boy called Aladdin. He lived with his mother, a seamstress, who worked very hard in a magnificent town in ancient Arabia. One day, Aladdin met a stranger waiting outside the door of Aladdin's house. The man was dressed in a great cloak and his head was covered by a turban.

"Tell me, boy, is your father's name Mustafah, the tailor?"

"Yes, sir, but he died a long time ago."

"I am your uncle and your father was my beloved brother. Every day I have mourned his disappearance," continued the man in the turban. He told Aladdin so many things about his father that the young boy ended up believing every word.

17

Sensing that Aladdin trusted him, his
uncle then said:

"Follow me to the mountain and
I will reveal my secrets to you."

Once in the mountains, Aladdin's uncle, who was an African
magician, lit a great fire, onto which he threw some magic perfume,
as he spoke magic words. Suddenly, the sun trembled and with a
terrifying rumble the earth opened. Aladdin bent down and saw
a big slab of stone with a metal ring set into it. Seeing Aladdin
looked frightened, the magician said to him:

"Don't be afraid, nephew. Under this stone lies a treasure that
will make you the richest man in the world. Pull the ring!"

Aladdin pulled the ring and the slab lifted to reveal a staircase.

"Go down!" ordered the magician. "When you come to a magnificent garden, you will find another staircase. Climb it and you will find a lamp, which you must bring back to me."

As Aladdin still hesitated to go down the stairs, the magician gave him a ring and added:

"Take this ring, it will protect you."

Aladdin put the ring on his finger and stepped down the staircase into the dark cave.

Soon he found himself in an extraordinary garden, where the branches of the trees were covered in rubies, opals, emeralds, and diamonds. Then he found the second staircase and, at the top, he came upon a wonderful, shining lamp. Aladdin picked it up, hid it under his shirt and returned the way he had come.

The magician was waiting for him at the top.

Aladdin held out his arms to
be helped out of the cave.

"Give me the lamp!" replied the
magician harshly.

"First help me out!" said Aladdin.

"You will not get out unless you give
me the lamp!" hissed the magician.

As Aladdin refused, the magician
turned red with fury and cast a spell
so that the heavy slab closed and
Aladdin found himself trapped
in the cave.

For three days Aladdin
neither ate nor drank.
On the fourth day he accidentally rubbed the
ring that the magician had given him. At that
moment, a huge genie appeared with twinkling
eyes. His booming voice echoed through the cave:
"I belong to you, oh master. What do you
want? Speak and I will obey you."

"Get me out of here!" begged Aladdin.
Immediately, he found himself outside
again, alone in the mountains. Once home,
Aladdin found his poor mother in tears.

"My child, I have no more money to
buy anything to eat," she wept.

But Aladdin remembered he had hidden
the magician's lamp in his shirt.

"Don't worry, mother, tomorrow I will go
to market and sell my lamp. I am sure to get
a good price for it if I clean it well first."

Aladdin took out his lamp and began to polish it when, without warning … a huge genie appeared, even more alarming than the first. His eyes were as red as fire and his beard was as black as coal. Aladdin bravely spoke to him: "We're hungry, bring us something to eat."

The genie gave him a delicious meal served on a silver plate and then disappeared in a puff of smoke. Aladdin's mother gazed in wonder at the lamp, then she sat down to eat. From that day onward they never knew hunger again.

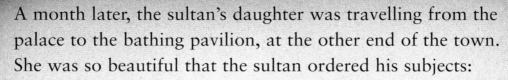

A month later, the sultan's daughter was travelling from the palace to the bathing pavilion, at the other end of the town. She was so beautiful that the sultan ordered his subjects:

"Stay at home. Close the shutters. No one must see my daughter."

But Aladdin got into the bathing pavilion and hid behind a column. When the princess arrived, she approached the bath and raised her veil. Then Aladdin could see her in all her beauty. Her eyes were enormous and full of kindness, and her shapely face was framed by her long brown hair.

Immediately, Aladdin fell deeply in love with the princess, and swore to ask the sultan for her hand in marriage the very next day. As soon as the sun had risen, Aladdin went to the palace. When he entered the throne room, he bowed respectfully to the sultan:

"Your Majesty, may I have the hand of your daughter?"

The sultan burst out laughing:

"How bold you are to come before me and make such a request! If you are so keen to marry my daughter, prove it by sending an army to be my personal bodyguard!"

Aladdin remembered the wonderful lamp and the genie. He rubbed the lamp and the genie soon appeared. "Genie, bring me an army of eighty soldiers on horseback and eighty men bearing sacks of silver and gold." At once the genie produced everything he had been asked. "Follow me to the palace!" the happy Aladdin ordered all the soldiers and men.

When they arrived at the palace, they were met by a joyful crowd. The men threw silver and gold coins to the onlookers who were cheering Aladdin on his way. Alerted by the noise, the sultan appeared on the palace steps and could not believe his eyes. He was so impressed by such riches that he immediately granted his daughter's hand to Aladdin.

The next day, Aladdin married the princess and the sultan gave the biggest party the kingdom had ever seen. The bride and groom set up home in a beautiful palace and lived there happily for many years.

Then, one day, the African magician learned that Aladdin was living in a magnificent palace with a beautiful princess. He returned to Arabia once more for the wonderful lamp.

Carrying a basket full of shining new copper lamps, he paraded under the palace windows shouting temptingly:

"New lamps for old! It's a bargain."

When the princess heard the magician's call she went out with Aladdin's old lamp in her hand. Recognizing the lamp, the magician seized it and rubbed it in his palm. Immediately the huge genie rose before him, bowed, and awaited his orders.

"Take me far away with the princess and her palace," cried the magician.

Then the palace, the princess, and the magician flew off to Africa, leaving Arabia far behind. Later when the sultan sent for his daughter, he discovered she had disappeared. Furious, he summoned Aladdin.

"What have you done with my daughter, you villain?"

Aladdin tried to explain that he knew nothing about the kidnapping of the princess. The grief-stricken sultan would not listen to him.

"Bring her back to me immediately or I will cut off your head!"

"Your Majesty, give me forty days to bring her back," begged Aladdin.

"Agreed," replied the sultan. "But if you have not brought back my daughter in forty days, you will die a horrible death."

In despair, Aladdin left the palace. What could he do to find his beloved princess? Then he remembered that long ago the magician had given him a ring for protection. He rubbed it and at once the genie who had released him from the cave appeared.

"I belong to you, oh master. What do you want? Speak and I will obey you."

"Help me once more, my good servant. Take me to my princess who has disappeared."

The genie gathered Aladdin in his arms and soon Aladdin found himself in Africa, right in the middle of the Sahara, where he saw his palace.

The genie set Aladdin down in front of the princess's door and gave him a magic bottle.

When she saw her husband again, the princess threw her arms round his neck.

"Aladdin, forgive me. It is all my fault. I exchanged your old lamp for a new one…"

She began to weep, but Aladdin comforted her:

"Do not worry, my dear wife. We will get back the wonderful lamp and return home. This is what you are going to do: choose your finest clothes and prepare a feast for the magician. Serve the very best wine. Then pour the contents of this bottle into his glass so that he will fall asleep forever."

The princess followed Aladdin's instructions and invited the magician to a wonderful meal. Charmed by the princess's invitation, the magician ate fully and drank his glass of wine in one gulp.

He dropped into a deep sleep. Aladdin came out of the cupboard where he had been hiding and took back the wonderful lamp.

He stroked it with his hand and the genie appeared.

"Take us home, powerful genie. To the sultan's country, and quickly!" he ordered.

The palace rose into the air and flew off toward Arabia. Aladdin and his princess gazed in wonder as countries and oceans passed beneath them. The genie set down the palace in its former place. Wild with joy, the sultan ran to his daughter and hugged her tenderly. Then he begged Aladdin to forgive him and ordered a month of rejoicing to celebrate the couple's return.

They both lived happily in their palace and had many children, who were the most beautiful ever seen in the country. As for Aladdin, he swore always to take great care of his wonderful lamp and magic ring.

THE END

History of Cinderella

The origin of the "Cinderella" is unknown. The earliest dated story was published in a Chinese book written by Tuan Ch'eng-shih around 850–860 CE in which the poor girl is called Yeh-Shen. Within this version there is no fairy godmother, but Yeh-Shen has a magical fish to help her instead and the glass slipper is a golden shoe.

In 1634, the earliest European version was published in Italy. In 1697, the Frenchman Charles Perrault published the version of the story we know today. The fairy godmother, the pumpkin that turns into a carriage, and the glass slipper are all mentioned in this version.

In the 19th century the German authors The Grimm Brothers wrote "The Ash Girl" which is based on the Cinderella story. This version does not have a fairy godmother. The poor girl plants a tree on her mother's grave, which gives her a magic dove and gifts to help her. The tree also takes revenge on the stepsisters by sending birds to attack them. In versions written by various other authors, the stepsisters have been turned to stone or even killed. Today's story is very kind to the two proud sisters.

In some versions of the tale, the Prince captures the Cinderella's slipper after he puts a sticky substance onto the stair to stop her running away, but Cinderella manages to free herself except for one slipper. Cinderella once again transforms into the beautiful princess with her rich dress and elegant hair as soon as the lost glass slipper is put on her foot.

Since then, Cinderella has become one of the world's most popular fairy tales with hundreds of versions published in books, performed on the stage, and watched as movies. There are possibly over a thousand versions throughout the world.

The moral of Cinderella seems to be that good things are more likely to happen to people who are good and kind, and who work hard.

History of Aladdin

"Aladdin" is a famous medieval Arabian story from the Middle East. In early versions of the tale, the story is set in China and Aladdin is a Chinese boy.

In 1710, this tale was included in *The Book of One Thousand and One Nights*, which was a collection of Arabic, Persian, and Indian myths and legends. The translator of the tales heard "Aladdin" and the story of "Ali Baba and the Forty Thieves" from an Syrian storyteller in Paris, France, and decided to include them in his book. The version written in 1710 is similar to the one we know today, except that, in the older tale, Aladdin uses the genie's wishes unwisely to become rich and powerful, but he doesn't realize that everything he has wished for—the riches, his castle, his wife—will be handed over to the sorcerer. Aladdin has to work with a less powerful genie to fight the sorcerer.

Genies are mythological creatures from the Middle East and Africa, and are also known as jinn (Arabic for genie) or djinn. They were evil spirits of the air that could take the form of any living creature. They were said to have magical powers and to grant wishes to anyone who would sell their soul in return. In ancient Rome, a spirit called a genius was thought to watch over a person, a bit like having a fairy godmother. In fact, genii (the plural of 'genius') were said to have wings. On a person's birthday, a genius was offered cake among other good things. The ancient Greeks had daemons instead of genii, who guarded over them.

Since then, Aladdin has become a hugely popular tale in books, theater productions, and movies.

The story shows that quick thinking and courage shines through whether you are a princess or a poor seamstress's son. Aladdin thought quickly and cleverly to work with the people and magic items around him to outwit the evil magician.